GABBY "THE GHOST" GILLESPIE

GABBY "THE GHOST" GILLESPIE

Tamarie Lynn Hart

authorHOUSE®

AuthorHouse™
1663 Liberty Drive
Bloomington, IN 47403
www.authorhouse.com
Phone: 1-800-839-8640

This is a work of fiction. All of the characters, names, incidents, organizations, and dialogue in this novel are either the products of the author's imagination or are used fictitiously.

Published by AuthorHouse   12/14/2012

ISBN: 978-1-4772-9967-8 (sc)
ISBN: 978-1-4772-9968-5 (e)

Any people depicted in stock imagery provided by Thinkstock are models, and such images are being used for illustrative purposes only.
Certain stock imagery © Thinkstock.

This book is printed on acid-free paper.

DEDICATED TO MY BEAUTIFUL GIRL, SAGE,

WRITTEN IN MEMORY OF MARIA

CONTENTS

INTRODUCTION

Try to remember as far back as you can; where you lived, things you did from day to day, your parents and other family members, and especially your house. Do you remember the dreams that scared you? What put fear in you to the point you could not scream? Did anything happen to you that you could not explain?

Commonly, young children and even babies have memories that stay with them forever.

I have memories of being in my crib. I was about two, I think, and sometimes I was afraid of the dark; not so much of the dark itself, but of what was in the dark. My mom would sit me in my crib in the evening, turn off the light, and close the door behind her.

It was hot and stuffy in my room and I would cover my head with my blanket anyway. I didn't like looking into the room because of the shadows and dark corners. If I stared hard enough, I could see figures of monsters coming out of their hiding spots. For fear of being eaten, I would breathe very quietly and not move a muscle.

Finally, after what seemed like hours, I just wanted to breathe fresh, cool air. I poked my nose and lips out from under the blanket, and aahhhh . . . as sweat ran down the sides of my forehead. The wanting of cool air against my skin overpowered the paralyzing fear of the monsters. Throwing the blanket aside, my eyes slowly adjusted to the dark, and then I saw him.

There! A tall figure stood at the foot of my crib, staring at me. I don't know how I knew he was staring, as I couldn't see any eyes. I just knew not to be afraid of him, whoever he was.

It wasn't my dad, because he was out in the kitchen talking to Mom. I knew it wasn't my brother, because he's not that tall and I could hear him snoring in his room across the hall. I remember the feelings of relief and calmness that replaced my fear, and I slowly closed my eyes and fell asleep.

It's amazing how, even as babies, we have a natural sense of what to fear and what not to fear. We just accept things as though we somehow remember places, people, and situations from say . . . another life? How else can explain the child prodigies of the world throughout history? As we grow up, we are conditioned to disregard and disbelieve things that cannot be scientifically proven. We are told to believe, depending on our culture, the beliefs of our parents, teachers, clergy, and other people of influence.

This is a story about a spirit energy named Gabby Gillespie. He is a mischievous and lonely entity that has attached himself to an old farmhouse in the Midwest. A young girl befriends him, and her mother manages to open up his life story. Some of the events in this story are based on true experiences.

Believe what you will, but I would be willing to bet that each of you readers, at one time or another, have had a story to tell; something that could not be explained; something you buried deep into your memory, guarding it as though it were the secret that would declare you insane.

Blocking it from escape, denying yourself to remember keeps you in your safe zone. Is that why we humans only use a small percentage of our brains? To keep safe?

What would it take us to truly open our minds, to accept things that do not always make sense? To explore the vastness of the universe and all its possibilities, material and nonmaterial.

Dare you remember? -

CHAPTER ONE

Sage's Room

It was a hot and sweltering July afternoon when I decided to climb the steep steps to my daughter's room, my hands balancing all the supplies I would be needing. Not far behind me was my Siamese cat, Maria. As I reached the top step, I felt the blast of heat. All the windows were closed and the air hung motionless and heavy. I pushed open the door to her room, and despite the heat I felt a chill on my neck and down my arms. My skin tingled and I felt all goose bumpy. *OK, there cowuld be some action in here,* I thought. Maria jumped gracefully onto the bed and immediately curled up for a little nap. I burned some sage in an abalone shell to smudge the room to "clear" any negative energy that might be there. The fragrant smoke hung in the air as I lit my white candles. Sitting in a comfortable position on the bed, I began reciting the "Prayer for the White Light of Protection."

Jeez! Why didn't we have air conditioning up there?! It was hard to concentrate on getting comfortable when sweat was running down my face and into my eyes. Shoulda brought up a towel with me! Ok . . . deep breath, through my nose and out my mouth . . . another . . . relax . . . breathe . . . deep breath . . . and out . . . oh shit! That was quick! I already felt eyes boring into the side of my neck. The hair on my arms stood up, my bowels churned, and I slowly turned to look to my left. Through the smoke still hanging in the air, I saw two glowing eyes staring straight at me. I recognized those eyes. Yes, they were the eyes of . . . Maria, my damned cat! She just squinted at me and twitched her tail. I hadn't even noticed when she jumped down off the bed and up onto some boxes in the far corner of the room.

Irritated, yet relieved, I tried to pick up my meditation where I left off. Closing my eyes again I breathed deeply and tried to clear my mind. This is harder to do than one might think. Christ! It's hot in here! Maybe I should try this another time, on a cooler day. I'm sweatin' my ass off, I'm gettin' a little crabby, and my cat thinks I have lost all sense of reality. No! Shut up! You're gonna do this . . . today. Stop making excuses, and just do it! I was always really good at telling myself off, and this was no exception. I used my shirt to wipe off my face, took a deep breath, and closed my eyes.

CHAPTER TWO

The Old Lethe Farm

Cyril and Delores Lethe and their children lived in the old farmhouse now. Standing majestically on top a big hill, just off County 5, you could see that much work was done here. Built around 1900, the main house saw many seasons and withstood generations of the Lethe family. In the Midwest, if you grew up on a farm, chances are your father, grandfather, and his grandfather grew up on the same farm. Over the years, buildings and additions were constructed to accommodate the growing livestock and families as well.

Seasons came and went here in the north country, bringing with them astounding beauty to the landscape. Springtime brought out the first colors of the year in the form of tulips and crocuses. Baby animals scampered around exploring their new world. The cold, fresh air was filled with the music of nature. The smell of green grass and black dirt was an intoxicating aroma that usually led to the beginnings of fieldwork and gardening.

As summer approached, the flowerbeds were planted with a wide variety and a rainbow of colorful annuals. Warm rains made the grasses lush, and the cornfields pushed forth their tiny little sprouts of green. Throughout the summer and into the fall was the time of year when a lot of work took place. Hard work usually involved almost every member of the family. Beginning in the early mornings and into the dark of night, there was always something that needed to be done. The bees buzzed and danced from one flower to another during the day, and the crickets and mosquitoes took over the nights. Apple tree branches hung low to the ground with their heavy burden of delightfully sweet apples. Hillsides exploded with colors from bright yellows to oranges, vibrant reds, and deep purples. Squirrels ran rampant, gathering nuts for their winter stashes, and most birds flew south to warmer climates. Harvest time was a flurry of activity for every farmer, all trying to beat the upcoming freeze. Fields were stripped of their bounty and hauled away by monster tractors and semi trucks.

Trees lost their leaves in the gusty winds of October, and they fell to the ground in a carpet of crispy layers. They would then be raked into piles and hauled to compost heaps for next year's garden, but not before the kids had the chance to run and jump headlong into the largest piles of leaves. A favorite was to burrow deep and then jump out at some passing member of the family, or better yet, a passing cat.

As the days grew shorter and colder, preparations for the long snowy winters included chopping wood and canning produce from the garden. The later months also signified the holidays of Thanksgiving and Christmas. Warming fires crackling in the fireplace set the mood for reflection and family togetherness. The first snowfalls of the season brought about all kinds of giddiness and excitement. Building snowmen and snow forts was a serious business and required much planning.

Sledding down long driveways was especially fun when the snow got packed solid.

The older kids would drag their sleds or pieces of cardboard out to the steep hills in the pastures. It's a wonder how any of them survived their childhoods, as at the bottoms of these hills were nothing but large trees and a dry creek bed.

The coldest nights made the snow crunch under their feet. Remember when Ma made you put empty bread bags over your socks to keep your feet dry? Pa spent long hours on his tractor with the bucket on the front, piling up snow from the driveway. These piles became their mountain, and many hours in sub-zero temperatures were spent playing a game called "King of the Mountain." The goal was simply to be the last person standing on top of the mountain. Sounds easy enough, but they were ruthless contenders. Bruises, bloody noses, black eyes, cuts, and scrapes were no deterrent in the quest of being named the "king."

But when chore time came around, they were all equals again, each doing their part in taking care of all the animals. At night, after a delicious supper and a hot bath, heavy eyelids forced exhausted kids up to their bedrooms. The warm, soft beds with thick blankets enveloped each of them as they dreamt about the next day's strategy of winning the mountain. Ma would blow out the last candle and look out the large picture window. What she would see was the moonlit snow that looked like billions of tiny diamonds sparkling for as far as she could see.

The breathtaking beauty of every season was truly nature itself.

The year was 1965 in the month of July. The main house was surrounded by manicured lawns and several blooming flowerbeds. Apple trees and large oak trees scattered the property and stood next to the barns. The cows grazed quietly in the lush, green pastures or napped in little groups contentedly chewing their cud. The family dogs barked excitedly as they chased the youngest kids around the back yard. Momma cat licked and nursed her new litter in the seclusion of the hayloft. The calves were outside their own little barn, munching on hay still wet from the morning dew.

The sun was hot, and there was no breeze as the sweat began to soak through Cyril's blue work shirt. His arms of deeply tanned, leather-like skin glistened with perspiration and dirt.

Every so often, mowing next to the house, he could catch a whiff of one of Ma's special breads. This made his stomach growl loudly as he grinned at nothing in particular.

Delores was tending to the evening meal by picking fresh vegetables out of the garden. The potatoes were doing nicely this year, she thought as she loaded up her apron with as many as she could carry. She would have to send Kate out to pick some carrots and lettuce for their salads. She headed back to house and was greeted by the mouth-watering smell of roasting beef.

She busied herself with the chopping of vegetables. When Kate entered the kitchen with her T-shirt full, she dumped it all into the large sink and began rinsing and washing. Soon supper would be ready. In the meantime, Ma found the time to scrub the floors while Kate prepared the salads. With that finished, Kate and her mom both worked together to make two mouthwatering apple pies for dessert. Kate loved helping her mom; she was able to learn to cook, clean, bake, and do laundry. Kate was different from the other children; if she wasn't helping Ma, she was buried deep into books, reading about faraway places and people. Their adventures kept Kate dreaming about the day when she would be old enough to do some exploring herself. Something had to be better than spending her whole life on this farm.

Soon, the house filled up with the noise of trampling feet, arguments, and a little one crying because someone slammed his little hand in the door. The dogs came in too and flopped down in their usual places, panting loudly as their saliva dripped freely onto the floor. Pa came in last to find Ma standing in the kitchen door, scowling at the scene in front of her. Walking over to little Matthew, she ordered everyone to wash up for supper. She took Matthew into the kitchen and started running the cool water. She picked him up and set him on the counter next to the sink. When her arms were around his little body, he stopped crying and looked at Ma with big eyes and a tear-streaked face, his little chest hitching from crying so hard. She gently took his hand and held it under the cool water. She took a soft cloth and wiped his face and arms. By then, Matthew was smiling as she hugged him. His hand felt better and there wasn't any bleeding, but she still took a small Band-Aid and applied it gently to the sorest finger. This was like a rite of passage for Matthew, for now he could show off his real injury, one so bad it that required a Band-Aid from Ma! Matthew held his hand high up in the air with pride so that all the family members could see it.

Kate was busy filling all the glasses with milk as the rest of the gang scrambled to their places at the table. Delores cleared her throat once to signify that is was time for the mealtime prayer. Pa started, and the rest joined in with the reciting of the prayer: "Bless us O" Lord and these our gifts, which we are about to receive, from thy bounty through Christ our Lord. In the name of the Father, and the Son, and the Holy Spirit, Amen."

Everyone was famished, as usual, and dove into the food, chattering all at once. One loud sigh from Ma and silence took over. Frenzy was replaced by order and manners. Pa had a small grin on his face as he quietly ladled up some gravy for his potatoes.

With the table cleared and the leftover scraps in the dog dish, Ma dished up the best warm apple pie they had ever tasted. It was topped off with a huge scoop of vanilla ice cream and drizzled with warm caramel sauce.

The evening ended with Kate helping the young ones with their baths while Ma and Pa took their steaming hot cups of coffee out to the front porch. The older boys came outside too, arguing about little things like whose turn it was to feed the cats or when the best time to unload hay would be.

Full stomachs and exhaustion soon took each of them over, and one by one, the boys filtered into the house to take hot showers and go to bed.

Ma and Pa went inside as soon as the mosquitoes started to come. Ma sat in her chair and picked up her knitting while Pa sat in his and pretended to watch the news. Smiling, Ma could hear the soft snoring as she covered him with a light blanket. He'd get up later to check on the animals before retiring to bed for the night.

CHAPTER THREE

Blaze!

Ma dreamt of bright, sunny afternoons filled with the delightful smell of freshly mown grass mixed with the acrid, choking smell of burning wood. Outside, the wind picked up as the sky grew black and lightning crashed into one of the oak trees next to the big barn, instantly shredding the entire tree and sending a shower of hot sparks. The thunder was deafening and actually shook the house. At the same time, a gust of wind blew a branch, hitting the bedroom window. Startled, she bolted up in bed, her eyes flew open, and she saw a bright orange glow against the opposite wall from the window. Panic set in as she screamed, "Pa! We have a fire!" Pa jumped to his feet and jammed his legs into his jeans, wrestled to get his T-shirt on, and ran for the door. Ma had the Fire Department on the phone, and the boys were already outside in their pajama bottoms, looking toward the barn frozen with shock and disbelief. Pa raced to the calf barn in hopes of rescuing as many calves as he could. The intense heat was already too great, and he was driven back helplessly. The stench of burning fur and flesh filled the air by the time the fire trucks arrived. Pa will forever remember the sounds he heard that night, as he turned away in horror. Ma tried to gather the little ones into the house while Pa and the boys watched helplessly as the firemen drenched the fire with water. It wasn't long before it was silent, as the barn and calf barn collapsed with a fury of sparks and burning cinders. Pieces of burning ash fell from the sky, so the firemen stayed to make sure nothing else caught fire. After they finally left, Pa shakily walked to the front porch and sat down. Placing his rough, hard-worked hands over his face, he cried. Ma came out of the house and onto the porch behind him. With a pained heart she approached him and put her hands on his uncontrollably shaking shoulders. She reached for his hand, and he grasped it with the strength of a drowning man. They clung to each other until just before sunrise. Ma thought to herself that she could never find a Band-Aid big enough for this hurt. The boys sat nearby, not making one sound except for the occasional sniffle and sob. They were just now realizing what had just been lost. The days following the devastating fire seemed dreamlike, with everyone adjusting to how much of their lives have changed. It seemed to Ma that her whole family had somehow evolved spiritually. What used to be taken for granted was no longer. This was a time of changes.

The boys grew up and went off to different colleges and universities. Kate was just starting senior high school, and the younger boys were now in one sport or activity after school. Pa rented out the land to crop farmers, and life just continued on. At least he was still able to keep the grounds around the house looking tip-top. I was hard for him to look toward where the barns once stood, so he let the grass and weeds grow up around the foundations as if to hide them.

Several years passed by as all the younger boys went off to different colleges and universities. The older boys all held jobs and had families of their own. Kate married her high-school sweetheart, Robert, and was expecting their first baby, due in the fall. Ma was excitedly knitting little baby blankets and booties, shopping for baby clothes, and planning the baptism. The whole family would religiously unite for the holidays and other special occasions. The years were filled with weddings, graduations, birthdays, and baptisms.

The Lethes decided to build a new house on the same property, one that would fit their much smaller family. The old farmhouse finally stood empty for the first time since it was built. The empty rooms seemed to echo with the distant sounds of the past. If you walked into the house, there was a crushing silence and the heavy feelings of sadness and loneliness.

The Lethes decided to rent out the farmhouse to help pay for some new furnishings for the new house. It was only a short time after they placed a FOR RENT sign at the end of the driveway when they began receiving inquiring phone calls from prospective renters. Ma released a long sigh while hoping that the new renters would take care of her home as well as she had.

CHAPTER FOUR

Moving Day

Moving from the city to the farm was a good choice for our family. Being raised on farms ourselves, Mark and I felt that this was exactly what we wanted. Sage, not so much. She was saddened and angry about having to leave her friends behind. Then we expected her to go to some stupid old school in the fall. Mark and I tried our best to console her and tell her how fun it would be when she met her new teachers and other students. This only sent her howling and bawling about how unfair life was. The drama was short-lived. When she heard us talking about the neighbors who just happened to have twin girls right about Sage's age, she came back into the room and sniffed, "Really?" We knew that she would adjust just fine when we saw that she made a fast and loyal friend in the Lethes' dog, Simone.

Simone was a huge black and tan Rott that looked as though she could separate your head from your shoulders at any given second. Turned out that she was just a big baby! She loved her having her tummy rubbed, and to express her gratitude, she would cover the nearest face with big, wet, slobbery kisses. She had to be the fastest face-licker this side of the Mississippi! Simone readily took to her new, self-appointed job of chasing and following Sage wherever she went. In turn, Sage would follow old Cyril Lethe wherever he went outside. Chatting and giggling, she made fast friends with him and Delores both. Cyril would keep her busy picking up apples off the ground that were still good and taking them in to Delores.

CHAPTER FIVE

Sage And Her New Friend

After settling into the house, we began to notice something with Sage's behavior. She was holding conversations with an "invisible" friend. Well, we thought this was probably normal since she was obviously upset about the move. This behavior would pass and she would adjust to her new surroundings, or so we thought. She also had the entire summer to get used to the idea of going to a new school.

If we had to go anywhere, she would let "him" into the back seat beside her, reach around "him," and fasten the seatbelt. We couldn't even start the car until she was satisfied that he was ready and comfortable. When she took her bath in the evening, she would sing and carry on quite lengthy conversations with "him." If I had to scold Sage about anything, she would cry and then sit off on her own and tell "him" all about it.

I started to get concerned when she started waking up in the middle of the night scared and upset because "he" wouldn't let her sleep. I tried talking to her, but she just burrowed deep between Mark and me. Each night was the same scenario. The argument, the refusal to sleep in her room, the crying, the pleading. Soon she was crawling into our bed every night. Genuinely, she was terrified of her room.

On one particular afternoon, she was in the room at the top of the steps, playing with her many dolls. There was a little play area, a bed with a dresser and a table. The room was well lit through two windows that faced west.

Mark and I were sitting in the living room downstairs watching television. I soon heard Sage's footfalls coming down the steps . . . fast. She ran into the living room and landed in my lap. Her breathing was very rapid and her heart was racing. Her eyes were large as she tried to tell us what had just happened. I tried to calm her down, because neither Mark nor I could understand anything she was talking about. After a few minutes, she finally explained that there were two girls in her room; they looked like sisters, one taller and the other smaller. They both looked at Sage and called her "Mom." That's when Sage ran down the steps. I asked Sage what they were wearing. She replied that they had on long pajamas with funny hats on their heads. She also said that the little one was carrying a little brown teddy bear.

I continued to hold Sage until she was calm again, and then she announced that she wanted to go outside and play with Simone. Mark and I looked at each other with the same confused expression. Then, just like nothing had happened, she ran outside to chase down Simone, already forgetting about her recent spooky visitors. I took this time to go upstairs to the room at the top of the steps. I sat on the bed and looked around. I sat there quietly for what seemed like an hour. I closed my eyes for a while . . . nothing.

Other things began to happen, too. In the middle of the night, one of her toys would turn on by itself. It was one of those that you have to manually squeeze a paw or push on its tummy. One particular night, I woke to the sound of a television. I listened for a minute and could even tell what program was on. *OK, someone forgot to shut it off again,* I thought. Shuffling down the steps, through the house, and through the living room, I came to a stop about fifteen feet in front of the television set. It was off. A cool draft hit the back of my neck. I stood very still for a few minutes, turned, and went back upstairs. Just as I got settled back into bed, Sage rolled over and mumbled, "He always likes the television on . . ." and fell back to sleep. I found my comfy position and closed my eyes. My eyes snapped open, as I could hear the television again, loud and clear. I wasn't going down there again.

There was the usual moving of small items. There is nothing more frustrating than knowing you set your keys on the kitchen table, turning to grab something else, and then reaching for your keys, and they're gone. The next half hour is spent looking for them, only to find them right where you left them . . . on the table.

I think my most frightening experience came early one morning as I was leaving to go to work. When I say early, I mean it was still dark outside. I left the house and walked toward the garage. As I neared the rear of the Jeep, I froze in my steps. I could clearly hear the sound of a large dog, breathing loudly! It was coming from directly in front of the vehicle. I turned just my head for just a second and saw that Simone was sleeping in her usual spot beside the Lethes' garage. Listening, I heard toenails clicking slowly as it walked toward the driver's side of the Jeep. With adrenaline surging to my pounding heart, I heard a snuffling noise. I shot to the passenger side, jerked open the door, and jumped inside. I then scrambled over to the driver's side, started the engine, turned on the lights, and jammed it in reverse. I raced backward out of the garage, looking around me at the same time . . . nothing. There was the nothing out there!

CHAPTER SIX

Spirit Check

My mother came for a visit one winter night when I was just putting a new tablecloth on our dining room table. I placed a beautiful cut crystal bowl full of deep, red apples in the center. We sat down with a couple of large mugs of hot, steamy cocoa and chatted about what has been going on in her life. Suddenly, she looked directly into my eyes and asked me if I had checked the house for spirits yet. Just then, the bowl "hiccupped" and one of the apples popped up, bounced on the table once, and then dropped to the floor. My eyes must have looked like saucers, because Mom just smiled and nodded her head at me. I decided to tell her about all the things that had been going on in the house and with Sage since we moved in. Mom did not seem too surprised and calmly told me that she could feel that there were several spirits in the house. She told me that there were not any devious or malicious spirits here, just ones that stop by and visit sometimes to see what has been happening. She advised me to burn some sweet grass and sage with the windows cracked open a bit. Then she said I needed to hang some cedar leaves above all the doorways.

My mother and I are Native American, and we come from a long line of medicine people. She tells me about my great-great-great-grandfather, Raymond. He was a real medicine man who knew wonderful and interesting ways to use the things that nature provided for making his medicines. He practiced and taught my mother as much as he could before he passed away at the age of 107.

My mother talks of him fondly. She recalls him as being a very tall man, standing 6'7". She said he was the kindest and most gentle person who ever lived. He had big, smiling eyes that could instantly put you at ease. I found myself wishing I had known him.

CHAPTER SEVEN

Vortex

For some months I had been attending spiritual awareness and psychic development classes. I decided it was high time I spilled my guts to the group. With much hesitation and several odd glances from Vicki, our teacher, I cleared my throat. Vicki looked at me and smiled knowingly. I began explaining how I felt that our house may have paranormal activity. I described Sage's behavior since our move to the farm. The rest of the class grew very quiet and focused their attention on me and what I was saying. I have always been sensitive to being the center of attention. My face grew red, and I felt hot and sweaty as I stammered on about my big-bad-dog-in-the-garage incident.

Vicki solemnly spoke about the fact that, our house being located at a sort of crossroad that drew gathering or visiting spirits; a type of vortex, if you will. They would just sort of stop for a while and then continue on their way. I remembered thinking to myself at that point that I had never, ever told her where I lived. She didn't seem surprised at all about what I was telling her and the group. After some discussion, she was very direct and to the point about what I needed to do.

The next day, I told Mark about my class the previous night, and he gave me a very strange look. Mark is very grounded and levelheaded, as well as somewhat of a skeptic. OK, he's a great big skeptic who never really says much; though on that day he decided to tell me about an experience he had several days prior. His thinking was, why add to the madness by telling me something like this right away? He explained to me that one night he decided to go to bed early. He had just gotten into bed when he became suddenly aware of a glow in the room. He looked toward the ceiling and saw, hovering the corner, a ball of light. He watched it for several seconds before it shot straight across the room, went through the wall to the outside, and was gone. His reaction was to simply ignore what had just happened, roll over, and fall asleep. After hearing his story, I knew it was time.

CHAPTER EIGHT

Hello!

I sat on Sage's bed in the mid-afternoon heat. I wasn't quite sure what I was expecting to happen, but I was waiting for something. Tired and thirsty, I rested my head in my hands covering my eyes. Maybe I could "see" something . . . anything. Please show me something I can understand, I prayed. I focused harder and concentrated deeper, yet nothing was coming to me. Afraid of falling asleep, I opened my eyes and reached for my notebook and pencil.

I began to scribble on a blank page, nothing legible, just scribbles. Now the heat was really starting to get to me. I needed water, a nice, big, cold, bottle of water . . . something startled me, and my head snapped to the left to look at Maria as if she had done something.

Confused for a second, I glanced down at my scribbling and became very excited about what I was actually seeing. Very lightly, I could see the letters G . . . A . . . B . . . B . . . Y . . . Gabby? In my head, I asked if the spirit energy in this room was named Gabby. Suddenly, thoughts came flooding to me faster than I could write them down. In a matter of minutes, or was it hours, I was given answers to all my questions.

CHAPTER NINE

Gabby And Sam

Gabby Gillespie was the name of a young boy who had lost his parents in a tragic car accident. He was only six years old when he became a ward of the state. Eventually, it was decided he would be in the care of his aunt Carolyn who lived in Texas. Carolyn was a middle-aged divorcee with no children of her own. She lived in a rundown trailer park just outside of Durham. Gabby found her to be a cold and somewhat bitchy woman who liked her booze a little too much, so he kept to himself most of the time. He hated his school because the kids were mean and the teachers ignored him. This was fine with him; he preferred to be alone anyway. When he was at home, he spent a lot of time in his room thinking about his mom and dad. He missed them terribly and cried a lot. Months passed, and as boredom and depression gripped him, he became increasingly angry. His aunt was hardly ever home, not that he cared. When she did stumble home drunk, she brought with her some old drunk guy she picked up at a bar. The small trailer would soon fill up with the smell of smoke and stale beer. Gabby had to get out right now. He knew that it would only be a matter of time before she would drag this idiot into her bedroom. Then he would never get any sleep. She disgusted him. Before dawn, he would creep outside through his window and revel in the fresh air and freedom. This had become the norm for Gabby; he liked the feeling of exploring further and further away from that dump of a trailer. He thought to himself that one day he would just keep walking and never stop.

It was warm already this morning, and the dusty breeze made the leaves look dry. It had been several days since the last rainfall, so Gabby decided to walk down by the creek. He cut through the wide ditch and into the large grove of trees. There he found what looked like a very well-worn footpath. Gabby and his wild imagination welcomed this adventure. As he followed the trail, he made believe he was a foreign traveler looking for treasure. His watch became a compass, and he wrapped his T-shirt around his head like a headband. The winding path brought him to a wide, grassy clearing. He scanned the field for wild animals and other explorers. Gabby breathed deeply, closed his eyes, and smiled to himself. Looking at the sun's position in the sky, he guessed that it was about midday already. The other clue was his loudly growling stomach. *Food, must find food,* he thought. He knew that the creek was around here somewhere. Squinting his eyes toward the edge of the field, he thought he saw movement. Gabby's stomach twisted with anxiety and excitement as he headed cautiously across the field. As he drew near, the creek became visible. The water looked really low and smelled horrible. Something caught his eye, so he quickly crouched down behind some tall weeds. "What the hell was that?!" he whispered to himself. Being eaten by some wild animal was not his idea of exploring for treasure. Of course, he was sure that sort of thing actually happened all the time, back in the explorer days. Still he wished he had brought some type of weapon. He looked around where he was hiding and spotted a branch; he thought this would have to do. He started to stand up when he heard something that sounded like rustling footsteps not that far away. Without warning, it jumped over and through the weeds that Gabby was hiding behind. It hit him from the side with such force that it knocked the wind right out of his lungs. Shocked and dazed, Gabby tried to gain his footing so he could see what was lying on the ground just feet from where he landed. Groaning in pain and holding his leg was a boy! He seemed to be about Gabby's age, maybe younger. Gabby looked down at the straggly-haired kid with wide eyes as he tried to catch his breath. He was doubled over for just a moment when he heard the boy ask, "W-w-who are y-y-you?"

Gabby staggered backward and sat hard on the ground again. He looked at the boy and replied, "Hows about you tellin' me who you are first?"

The boy winced in pain as he slowly stood up. "M-m-m-my n-name is S-s-sam," he said, rubbing his leg.

"Well, S-s-sam, my name is Gabby."

"N-nice ta m-m-meetcha," said Sam, offering his dirty hand to Gabby. The boys shook hands and awkwardly looked around.

"So, what is this place?" Gabby asked.

Sam replied shyly, "I-im not s-sure. I j-j-just come h-here sometimes."

Gabby looked at Sam, and Sam nervously looked down at his feet with his hands jammed into his pockets. Sam glanced around and asked Gabby where he came from. "Ya mean, where do I live?" Sam shook his head. Gabby said, "Well, somewhere that way in a trailer park."

"I j-just live through those t-t-trees in a c-c-cabin, w-w-w-with m-my d-d-dad," Sam stuttered. Gabby's stomach growled loudly in protest, and Sam giggled.

"Hey! Ya wanna come to my place? I make a mean peanut butter sammy," Gabby exclaimed. Sam nervously looked around and shook his head yes. Like a shot, both boys made double time cross the field and up the dusty path. By the time they reached Carolyn's trailer they were red-faced and out of breath. Gabby made them stop as he turned to Sam with a finger over his lips. They crept to the door, and Gabby listened. With a sigh of relief, Gabby grabbed Sam by the shirt and pulled him toward the door. Once the boys were in the trailer, it was a free-for-all scramble for food. Leaving the kitchen as though a tornado had struck, they grabbed sodas and ran back outside. Both were giggling uncontrollably by the time they reached the gravel road that led to Sam's cabin.

"S-s-so, where was your M-mom?" Sam asked.

Gabby's face turned ashen, and he bluntly replied, "My mom's dead; my dad too."

"Uh . . . oh . . . s-s-sorry." Sam said.

"I hafta live with my aunt Carolyn fer a while." Gabby explained. "That's OK, though. She doesn't have a clue; she's drunk all the time." Sam nodded his head; he did understand about parents like that, only too well. They walked the gravel road for a few miles, just talking and kicking rocks along the way.

Soon it was beginning to get dark, and Sam was acting really nervous. "W-well, I b-b-better g-g-git to goin' h-h-home now. M-m-my d-dad will be th-there s-s-soon," said Sam quietly.

Gabby wondered why Sam didn't talk about his parents. *Oh well,* he thought, *Sam will talk when he feels ready.* "OK, Sam, see ya tomorrow?"

Sam just gave Gabby a shy nod, turned, and walked slowly toward the old cabin.

"Where the hell you been all damn day, ya little pisshead?!" yelled Daren as Sam stepped inside the cabin. Sam dodged a blow as he ducked around a fist meant for his face. Daren growled obscenities under his putrid, alcohol-smelling breath. Sam easily lunged past him and locked himself in his bedroom. He curled up on his bed and placed his headphones over his ears to drown out the ravings of his father's wrath. He knew he would either pass out in his chair at the kitchen table or stumble out the door and get in his old, rusty, beat-up pickup and drive to the nearest bar. By the time he arrived back home, he was falling down, struggling to get to the bathroom and not making it, a large, dark, wet pee stain covering the front of his grubby pants. Cussing, he grabbed another bottle of beer out of the fridge and sat heavily in his chair at the table again. This time, he'd only drink a couple sips before passing out cold. This relieved Sam immensely as he could now sleep himself. This time Sam felt fortunate; other times Daren went out of his way to pound the crap out of him.

Sam's mother had left them five years ago when Sam was only seven. She had enough of his father soon after he lost his job with the drilling company. Lisa tolerated Daren's abusive behaviors until one stormy night, leaving poor Sam to fend for himself. He remembered that night clearly. Daren was in a drunken stupor while she silently packed up her meager belongings. Lisa came into Sam's room and told him she was leaving. She kissed Sam's cheek, looked into his sad eyes, and said, "Baby, you need to be strong for me, OK? I love you, son, but I can't take you with me right now, OK? Stay here, and when I find another place, I will be back to get you, OK?" Sam looked at his mom, somehow knowing he would never see her again. He just looked at her with sad eyes and gave her a slow nod yes. She hugged him tightly, and with that she was gone. He watched her walk to the end of the grassy driveway, not once looking back. Sam wanted to run as fast as he could to go with her, so he jumped off the bed, grabbed a T-shirt, and ran to the door. Sam's heart sank as he saw his mom jump into a strange car and drive off. He watched the red taillights until they disappeared into the dusty distance. That was the last time he'd ever see her.

Long before Daren woke up to start drinking all over again, Sam was already waiting for Gabby at the path. He hoped they would do some more exploring today down by the creek. Gabby crept up on Sam to scare him and did just that! Sam let out a yelp and chased Gabby until they could run no more. Neither was sure where they were exactly or how long they'd been running. Sam looked around, confused, "I-i-i n-never went this f-f-far from m-m-my place b-before."

Gabby had to agree; he hadn't either. "Hey, don't worry, we'll find our way back," Gabby reassured Sam. The boys continued through a small grove of trees and found themselves at what looked like a deserted house. This house was huge and very old, and surely no one lived here. The driveway was covered with overgrowth; the fence surrounding the yard was made of wrought iron and was in very poor shape.

Sam said, "Y-you're not th-thinking what I think you-you-you're thinking."

Gabby had a smirk on his face, confirming Sam's reason for worry. "Come on!" shouted Gabby, as he took off through the broken gate.

"W-w-wait!" cried Sam.

"Ch-ch-chicken!" mocked Gabby.

The boys reached the front porch and slowly approached the door. The door was hanging by one hinge, and the glass in it was broken. They looked into all the windows on the lower floor to see if anyone was there. All there was to see were a bunch of stacks of old newspapers and magazines, dusty old furniture, tables full of books, and boxes full of stuff.

"Wow, look at all that cool stuff!" Gabby said with excitement. Sam just wrinkled his nose. "What, you wouldn't like to see what all that stuff is?"

Sam just shrugged his shoulders. He knew that if Gabby was going in, so was he, so why argue, right? Gabby tried the front door, and it swung open wide. Sam followed with much hesitation, but curiosity soon took him over. The air hung heavy with dust and the smell of musty furniture. Gabby and Sam explored every room, every closet, corner, and cupboard. In one of the boxes, they found a bunch of old pictures and some newspaper clippings.

Sam looked through the pictures while Gabby read the clippings. Neither boy knew the people in the pictures, so they carefully placed everything back in the box. They went about looking at the books stacked on one of the tables and found what looked like an old map tucked into the pages of one of them. The boys found this just too hard to resist. After examining it, they decided it had to be a treasure map.

Suddenly they heard a loud noise that came from outside. They hadn't thought that someone may actually be living here, which meant they were trespassing, which meant they needed to get the hell out of there! Gabby crammed the map into his pocket, and both boys ran to the back of the house. There was an open window where they crawled through and dropped to the ground with a thud. Scrambling to their feet, they stood up and came face to face with a large, bearded man holding a shovel. Sam froze, but Gabby took off like a shot toward the grove of trees. He turned to scream at Sam just in time to see the old man take a swing, barely missing Sam's head. The man was thrown off balance long enough for Sam to gain his footing and run to where Gabby was standing, face void of all color. Gabby nearly wet his pants waiting for Sam to catch up, and when he did, both boys sprinted into the trees. Without looking back, they ran until they were out of breath. Gasping for air, their legs could carry them no further, and they both rolled to the ground in a cloud of dust. A few minutes passed before they burst into uncontrolled fits of laughter, each turning red-faced with tears streaming down their dirty faces. Sam nervously looked back toward the old house and announced, "I-I th-think we might b-b-be f-f-far enough aw-w-way now."

Gabby looked at his friend's face and was hit by another fit of giggling. He replied, "You should . . . have seen your . . . face when that . . . old fart looked at us in a . . . heap on the ground! I could have just shit right then and there!"

"I th-th-thought you d-did!" laughed Sam. Gabby thought they should try to find their way back home, just in case Carolyn found her drunk ass home early. Sam agreed, suddenly looking preoccupied with his own worries.

They reached Sam's house to find Daren working on his piece-of-shit pickup. As the boys approached the cabin, he looked around the hood and snarled, "Where have you been, boy!"

Sam replied, "W-w-w-we were j-just explorin' the w-w-woods over th-there."

"Who's yer friend here?" Daren pointing a wrench at Gabby.

"My name is Gabby. I live just over there, sir."

"Did you just call me . . . sir?" asked Daren, now standing up. "Nobody calls me sir, you understand that? Now get the hell outta here, and you get inside and clean up the kitchen!" he yelled. Gabby waved at Sam, feeling sorry for his friend, and turned and headed to his own piece of hell.

The summer passed by quickly, and if it weren't for Sam, it would surely have felt like an eternity. He and Sam would spend day after day comparing their everyday run-ins with their drunk caregivers. Caregivers, hell, they were the ones needing the care. Too bad they just didn't get together themselves and have one big party that never ended. Sam and Gabby often planned what they were going to do when they were done with school. Like all childhood friends, they vowed to always be together and live in the same little town far away from there, of course. Find a good job and get married, if they had to; have kids that they actually loved, and grow old and die happy.

The summer was drawing closer to fall, and that meant the beginning of school. For some reason, though, Gabby noticed that Sam was being a little more anxious than usual. He just figured that his dad had been getting drunker than he normally did. He was right, as one day, Sam had not wanted to go home at all. He seemed to want to go exploring further and further and not turn back. Finally, Gabby convinced Sam that it would be OK and that the next day they would go far beyond where they had ever gone. They agreed to pack lunches and meet at the creek where they had first met, right at dawn. Sam reluctantly headed for the cabin where Daren waited.

Carolyn was at the kitchen table, smoking a cigarette, already in a fog of alcohol. As Gabby opened the door, she sneered in his direction with bleary eyes and told him to sit down. She had something to tell him. He sat down and listened while she told him he was to go live with her sister, Betty. Aunt Betty and Uncle Ed lived several hundred miles away, in another county. Gabby fought back angry tears as she glared at him. "Go on, ya little shit! Git yer stuff packed. We are leaving here by noon tomorrow!" Instead, Gabby ran out the door and headed back to Sam's.

Crossing through some back yards, he ran down the dusty gravel that led to the cabin. As he neared, he saw red and blue flashing lights everywhere. "Sam!" he screamed. He ran faster toward the lights. "Sam! Where are you?" Gabby's stomach twisted and turned with each footfall. Rounding the front of the waiting ambulance, his face turned white. Policemen and suits were milling around while ambulance workers prepared to lift a gurney that carried a small figure under a white sheet. As they lifted the gurney, Gabby saw a large red blood stain on the sheet as well as all over the ground beside the sidewalk that led to the cabin. Standing in the doorway was Sam's dad, struggling to stand up against the door jam. In his hand he held a baseball bat covered with what Gabby guessed to be his friend's blood. The police had their guns drawn as they tried to convince him to put down the bat. Finally Daren complied, and they swiftly threw him to the ground and handcuffed him. As they placed him in the squad, a suit approached Gabby as he stood in total shock and disbelief.

"Hi," he said. "My name's Jim. What is your name, son?"

Gabby weakly replied, "Gabby, sir."

Jim propped himself against the bumper of his unmarked and looked into Gabby's face. "Well, son, I'm real sorry about your friend; seems he caught the business end of a baseball bat. But don't worry, this looks like an open and shut case, you maybe should be . . ." Gabby ran blindly toward the trailer park. Out of breath, he stumbled into the trailer, pushing past Carolyn. Barely making it to the bathroom, he lost his stomach.

Gabby did not sleep that night; he kept thinking about poor Sam. Why didn't they leave and not come back, like they had talked about so many times? Why did he talk Sam into going home at all, knowing the evil that waited for him? He can't just be gone! God! Damn it! He can't be gone! Gabby's mind screamed.

The next day seemed a blur, like a nightmare that he just couldn't wake up from. By eleven o'clock, Carolyn was already impatiently waiting in her car, cigarette hanging out of her thin lips. Dark glasses covered her squinting, bloodshot eyes, and she still reeked of stale beer. Gabby threw his things into a bag when he heard the car start. His head pounded, yet the rest of him felt numb. He had no more than thrown his bag into the back seat when the bitch started backing out of the driveway. Gabby jumped in and took one more glance toward Sam's place. With painful resignation, he put on his headphones and laid his head against the window. The window felt smooth and cool as he quickly fell into a fitful sleep.

Gabby was rudely awakened by a hard slap to the top of his head and Carolyn yelling at him to wake the fuck up. Gabby opened his eyes as she took a hard turn into Ed and Betty Lethe's driveway. What he saw was a large white farmhouse with a nice big yard. Carolyn skidded to a stop and waited for Gabby to get out. At least she waited for him to grab his bag before jamming the car into reverse. Not saying a word, she left in a cloud of dust, no doubt to get back in a hurry so she could start drinking. Knowing he would not miss her in the least, he turned to approach the front door. Just as he reached for the doorbell, he heard someone from inside call out to him. "Come on in, Gabby! We've been waiting for you!" a woman's voice called.

CHAPTER TEN

A Knock On The Door

A small knock on the door snapped me back into reality. Sage plodded into the room and asked, "Whutcha doin'?" I just smiled at her and wondered how long I had been up there. The candles had long since burned out, and it was already dark outside. Before I left the room, I smiled and thanked Gabby for whatever he was doing to get me to understand his story. Quite happy with myself, I called my mom to tell her what I was able to do. She seemed happy to hear it, but at the same time she warned me of the possibility of increased activity. "Now you tell me this?" I asked nervously. I was now on high alert for anything to happen, though nothing did. Mark and Sage settled in to watch *The Wizard of Oz* together, but I decided I had seen enough of those damn flyin' monkeys. They scared the hell out of me. I figured that this might be a good time to try and pick up where I left off with Gabby, and I headed back upstairs. It was noticeably cooler up there as I lit some more white candles and re-smudged the room. This time, without Maria, I found my comfy spot and closed my eyes. I greeted Gabby in my mind and waited.

CHAPTER ELEVEN

Ed And Betty Lethe

"How are you, young man?" Uncle Ed asked as Gabby plopped down his bag. Gabby was somewhat disoriented and in shock from the recent horrific nightmare. His mind replayed over and over again the numbing scene at Sam's cabin. Anger grew inside him once again, and hot tears filled his eyes.

"Fine, sir," whispered Gabby, barely audible. Looking at the floor, he didn't notice that Betty had entered the room. She was a large woman in her mid-fifties with a cheerful, wide smile and green eyes. She was wearing a gray sweat suit with some powdery white stuff on one sleeve.

"Come on, son; let's go into the kitchen, huh?" Ed said.

Betty approached Gabby and gave him a big, soft hug that smelled of fresh-baked cookies and soap. He was in an instant swept into the past, when his mom got into one of her baking moods. She would let him help pour in the chocolate chips while she stirred the dough. He missed her so much, and his emotions were getting harder and harder to conceal.

"What's on yer mind, boy?" Gabby snapped back into the present and realized that he was kinda hungry. Betty handed him a cookie and poured him a nice tall glass of ice-cold milk. As they sat at the kitchen table, Gabby felt a little odd not seeing a single bottle of vodka or can of beer sitting beside an overflowing, stinking ashtray. *So this is what a normal kitchen smells like,* he thought to himself. Ed and Betty sipped hot coffee while Gabby devoured three cookies. He hadn't tasted anything this good in what seemed like forever. They sat and talked for a while about the school he would be attending in the fall. Gabby felt for the first time like he was where he belonged. Betty showed him around the house while Ed finished his coffee. Gabby, feeling a little better now that he had something in his stomach, suddenly felt exhausted. Sensing his fatigue, Betty showed him where his bedroom and bathroom were. She told him to take some time to clean up, unpack his belongings, and settle in. Before closing the door, she smiled at him and said she'd have dinner ready in a few hours. Gabby sat on his bed, took a deep breath, and closed his eyes.

The summer grew cooler as fall approached, which also signified the start of the new school year. Gabby experienced the usual anxiety that came with starting in a new school, but he knew that somehow he would live. His school was five or six miles away from where he stayed, which meant he would have to take the bus. Ed and Betty took him to the school a few weeks before it actually started so he could meet his new teacher. Mrs. Dunn seemed OK, he guessed, as long as she wasn't like the teachers at his old school. He didn't much care what the other kids were like; he didn't plan on befriending any of them. Since the harshness of losing Sam, he surely wasn't going to let anyone that close again. He thought of Sam often, remembering the past summer exploring. He suddenly thought about the map they found in an old book at that old house. He would never forget how hard he and Sam laughed about nearly getting caught by that old coot. His smile soon dissolved when he thought about Daren. He hoped that he was rotting in prison, so when he croaked, he could then rot in hell for what he did to poor Sam. He thought a moment of Aunt Carolyn, too. She called once in a great while to talk to Betty, but never once did she ask how Gabby was doing. Bitch.

Gabby stood at the front steps of his school, afraid to step inside for fear it was going to be just like the other school. *Well,* he thought to himself, *I'm not going to find out standin' out here just starin' at the door.* With that, he opened the door and stepped inside. He was just a few minutes late, so the halls were pretty empty. He found his way to his homeroom, took a deep breath, and walked through the doorway. Mrs. Dunn looked at Gabby as he entered and smiled, just glad he showed up. Gabby's face felt hot and grew red with embarrassment, "Sorry I'm late," he mumbled. His palms started to sweat as he stumbled to his seat toward the rear of the classroom. The girls giggled and the boys clapped and snorted back laughter.

He sat down in his seat with his ears burning and hands shaking. He took a deep, heavy sigh of relief and thought, OK, this is it. I made it this far and I'm still alive. Gabby glanced around the room and sized everyone up. He decided that maybe this wouldn't be too bad after all. The rest of the day passed uneventfully except for being approached by a weird girl from his homeroom. He didn't quite know what to make of her, but he guessed she was pretty nice just the same.

CHAPTER TWELVE

My Sweet Amy

She was smaller than the other girls in his grade, and she was different somehow. Gabby couldn't quite put his finger on it, but he tried not to care. Her name was Amy, and she wore her hair in two ponytails, sometimes braided, but always two. She had the deepest brown eyes he had ever seen. They seemed to be almost black, as black as her mood sometimes. Something about her made Gabby felt sorry for her. He was pretty sure it had something to do with her family; didn't it always? Amy sat next to him at lunch one day, but she didn't say one word. Gabby didn't push her either; he wasn't sure he wanted to know her. Yet something about her beckoned his attention, he couldn't deny. She seemed miles away most times, and that is what seemed to draw him to want to be near her more. *DAMN!* he thought. *DAMN, DAMN!* She was looking straight at him now. His stomach did a one-and-a-half twist as he decided to walk over to her and muttered, "Hi." She just looked at him with those deep eyes and walked away, saying nothing. The days that followed only resulted in more of the same reaction. Gabby thought, why should I even try? She's obviously some kind of a loner, like me, right?

That following winter, he decided to talk to her openly, not giving her the chance to run away from him. Amy surprisingly didn't walk away from him this time. She just looked him right in the eyes and asked, "So what's your problem? Why do you keep watching me? You're really startin' to freak me out."

Gabby was surprised at the toughness in her voice. It didn't seem to fit her stature at all, but he later learned that the tough exterior was merely her defense mask. Amy and Gabby eventually got to know each other; never had he put so much effort into getting to know someone. She didn't just have a wall around her—she had a fortress!

One afternoon, Gabby decided to ask her about her family, a question he regretted later. Amy withdrew as if he had just bitten her. Hard! She backed away scowling with what Gabby guessed was hot anger. "Don't you ever ask me that again! That's none of your damned business, you hear me?" she cried.

She stayed far away from him for about a month after that. Gabby couldn't believe her stubbornness! He thought hard and decided to confront her. "Am I your friend?" Gabby asked her one day.

She shook her head as she apologized for her overreaction.

"Do you trust me, Amy?" he continued.

She struggled with her answer but replied, "Yes."

They agreed from that point on that they would talk things out, as they both admitted that they missed each other. Gabby felt himself grow closer to her with each passing day. He noticed that she had missed a few days of school, but he decided not to be nosy. One day, in the early spring, she came to school late, but that's not what bothered Gabby the most. It was her hair . . . she wore it down over one side of her face. Amy tried to avoid facing him, but he cornered her by her locker anyway. He knew that something was very wrong when she wouldn't face him right away. His heart sank when she slowly turned and looked at him with red, swollen eyes. His concerned soon turned to white-hot anger when he noticed the large, purple bruise on her left cheek. She didn't need to explain anything to him; he knew by her crushed spirit and pleading eyes. Gabby silently knew her secret, and it all made perfect sense now. He had to keep his cool. He didn't want her to pull away again; it took him too long to gain her trust. On his way home that afternoon, his mind wandered back to the day he lost

Sam. Gabby was damned if he was going to just sit back and let something bad happen to Amy. This can't happen to her, not his Amy. His fondness for her even surprised him as he vowed to protect her from her monster. His stomach flip-flopped as he devised his plan for that very night. He had to see for himself; he would see exactly who did this thing to her.

Ed and Betty usually went to bed fairly early, and Gabby found his opportunity to slip quietly out his window. He couldn't tell them anything right now; they would only try to stop him from getting involved. He knew he was hell bound on a fast track to get to her house. The night was dark as he crept into her yard, yet there were several trees and bushes to duck behind if he needed. Now he just needed to find Amy's bedroom window; he had to know she was OK. The house was dark from the front, so he decided to check the rooms at the back of the house. He noticed a faint glow coming from one of the windows, and he slowly made his way to just below it.

The sounds he heard coming from the closed window made him sick to his stomach. "Oh, please, God, don't let this be Amy's room, please, please . . ." He felt like he had lead weights on his shoulders as he raised up tall enough to see inside the dimly lit room. Gabby's eyes adjusted to the lack of light, and his fears were confirmed in an instant. Hot bile rose in his throat as he witnessed the horror of a pasty, sweaty, overweight man huffing and humping, trying to force himself into the small, helpless girl he recognized as Amy. He caught a glimpse of her terrified face, mouth open in a silent scream. Tears streamed from her eyes in unbearable pain. Her hair was knotted and wet as she lay pinned under the massive weight of her father. Gabby was so blinded by anger that he found it hard to breathe. He stumbled back around to the front of the house and without hesitation burst through the door.

"Get off her, you fuckin' rat bastard!" Gabby screamed into the darkness. "Get the hell off her!"

Amy's father jerked with surprise and pulled himself away from Amy. He grabbed her by the throat and slammed her into the wall. "I'll be back, you little slut!" Dizzy with pain, she slid down the wall in a small whimpering heap. Stan was a large man, and he was pissed off as he stomped into the living room where Gabby stood his ground. He yelled, "Who the hell are you?! You little freak, come 'ere!"

Stan didn't see the fireplace poker that the intruder held behind his back. Gabby took a few steps back and waited for the monster to rush at him. Bellowing like a bull, Stan did exactly what Gabby wanted him to do. With arms out in front of him, he lunged at Gabby at good speed. The next thing he knew, he had the cold iron poker lodged deep into his upper thigh. The blood looked black as it sprayed from Stan's wound. The look of pain and surprise took him over as he slowly sunk to the floor. Gabby only wished that the poker was red hot and that his aim was just a little bit higher and to the left a smidge.

He jumped over Stan lying in a growing pool of blood to find Amy's room. Gabby rushed down the hallway, ""Amy! . . . Amy?! Where are you?" He heard faint sobbing, and he frantically opened the door to her room. He found her in the corner, and his heart felt like it was being crushed. Quickly and effortlessly he scooped her up and gently placed her on the bed and wrapped her in a blanket. Her hair hung in snarls over her face. She was shaken, hurt, and scared. He quietly held her, wishing he had been there sooner.

Gabby called 911, which brought the police, ambulance, and Fire Department. He knew that he would be arrested for breaking and entering, assault with a deadly weapon, and probably attempted murder, but he didn't care. Amy would get the help she so desperately needed. She was taken to the hospital where she agreed to have DNA tests performed to prove that her father had been molesting her. She was assigned a social worker and placed in a county home. Stan survived his attack but was being held in the county jail until his court date.

Ed posted Gabby's bail of $25,000.00, and he was released into the custody of Ed and Betty. Gabby's attorney, Mr. Adolph, was able to keep him from being tried as an adult.

Stan was found guilty and sentenced to fifteen years in the state penitentiary. He was killed just three years later by a fellow inmate; you see, even other scum do not tolerate rapists or, worse, child molesters. Gabby's case went to court early that summer, but it was short lived. Amy's testimony showed that he acted in self-defense and mostly to rescue her from her father. Gabby was acquitted on all charges and released into the custody of his aunt Carolyn, with only six months probation. Judge Thomas thought it best if Gabby didn't stay in the immediate area. Ed and Betty took the news with disappointment but understood the reasoning. Amy was saddened by Gabby's having to leave but was forever grateful to him for coming into her life and freeing her from her prison of pain. She really never was the same again, but she graduated from high school anyway. A struggle with depression and PTSD led her to abuse drugs. Amy was eventually found dead of an overdose at age nineteen. By the time Gabby heard of her death, he was already well on his way to being addicted to alcohol. Thanks to Carolyn's never-ending supply of booze. Gabby withdrew into himself more and more with each year that passed.

Carolyn's boozing only worsened as now she just sat at her table, mumbling incoherently in a cloud of smoke and a half-empty can of beer. Gabby also found solace in the bottle and traveled the path to destruction without regret. On the evening of his twenty-first birthday, he drank until he could drink no more. Clutching an old photograph of his parents, he passed out in his dark little bedroom. By three AM he had drowned in a pool of his own vomit. Carolyn discovered him days later when she began noticing a rotten smell coming from the back of the trailer. When she opened the door to Gabby's room, she was hit by the gagging stench of death. Gabby was laid to rest next to his parents in the small church cemetery where he had spent his childhood. On his grave marker there was a quote that read:

Carry me home on the wings of a dove, so I can be with the ones that I love.

CHAPTER THIRTEEN

Gabby's Choices

Things don't always work out the way you want them to, and Gabby wouldn't cross over into the light that would lead him home to his mother, father, Sam, and Amy. He kept wandering this earth and was hopelessly drawn to the old Lethe farmhouse. There, a girl full of life and love, with parents who cherished her, is what anchored his spirit to that place. He hadn't meant to make her afraid of her room; he just wanted to play and experience her life with her. I felt the sadness that was falling over him and decide to make him a deal.

If he would let Sage sleep at night in her room, in her own bed, he could stay for as long as he wanted. But I also told him that if he would only move into the light that was waiting for him, he'd find the immense love of God, the unyielding comfort and serenity of being "home." He would also finally be reunited with his loving parents, Sam, and Amy. This seemed hard for Gabby to resist, as I felt the tug of war going on in his soul.

I asked, "What can I do to help you?" Moments passed, and the silence grew heavy as I closed my eyes. In an instant I saw a clear image, a perfect image of a ghost, you know, like Casper? I was suddenly hit by a rush of ideas.

Gabby wanted to be around happy people. He wanted to experience the unconditional joys of a real family. Gabby then hit me with another image. It was a big, yellow, happy face!

I knew then and there what he wanted me to do, and it also meant that he was going to go home. With that, his energy was gone. *Meet you on the other side, Gabby,* I thought to myself.

I wasn't aware of how late it was, just that Sage was sound asleep in Mark's lap. His head was tipped back and he was softly snoring as I covered them both with a light blanket. I smiled at them and went to bed myself. I had a lot of thinking to do.

THE END

ABOUT THE AUTHOR

Tamarie Lynn Hart was born in St. Paul, Minnesota. A member of the Red Lake Band of Chippewa Indians, she lives in a small community in southeastern Minnesota. There she and her husband, Mark, raise their granddaughter Sage. Tammy began writing poetry, and then the idea for this book started to materialize.

She is also a hot-glass artist and jewelry designer. The beads that she makes go into some of her jewelry pieces.

I want to express my heartfelt gratitude to Mr. Julius Petersen of Denmark, a retired teacher and valued friend for teaching me how to believe in myself and to how to trust again. With his help I also learned the valuable concept of patience. Thanks my friend, this book is also in your honor.

Printed in the United States
By Bookmasters